ALL THINGS
D1174178

SAM BAKER, GONE WEST

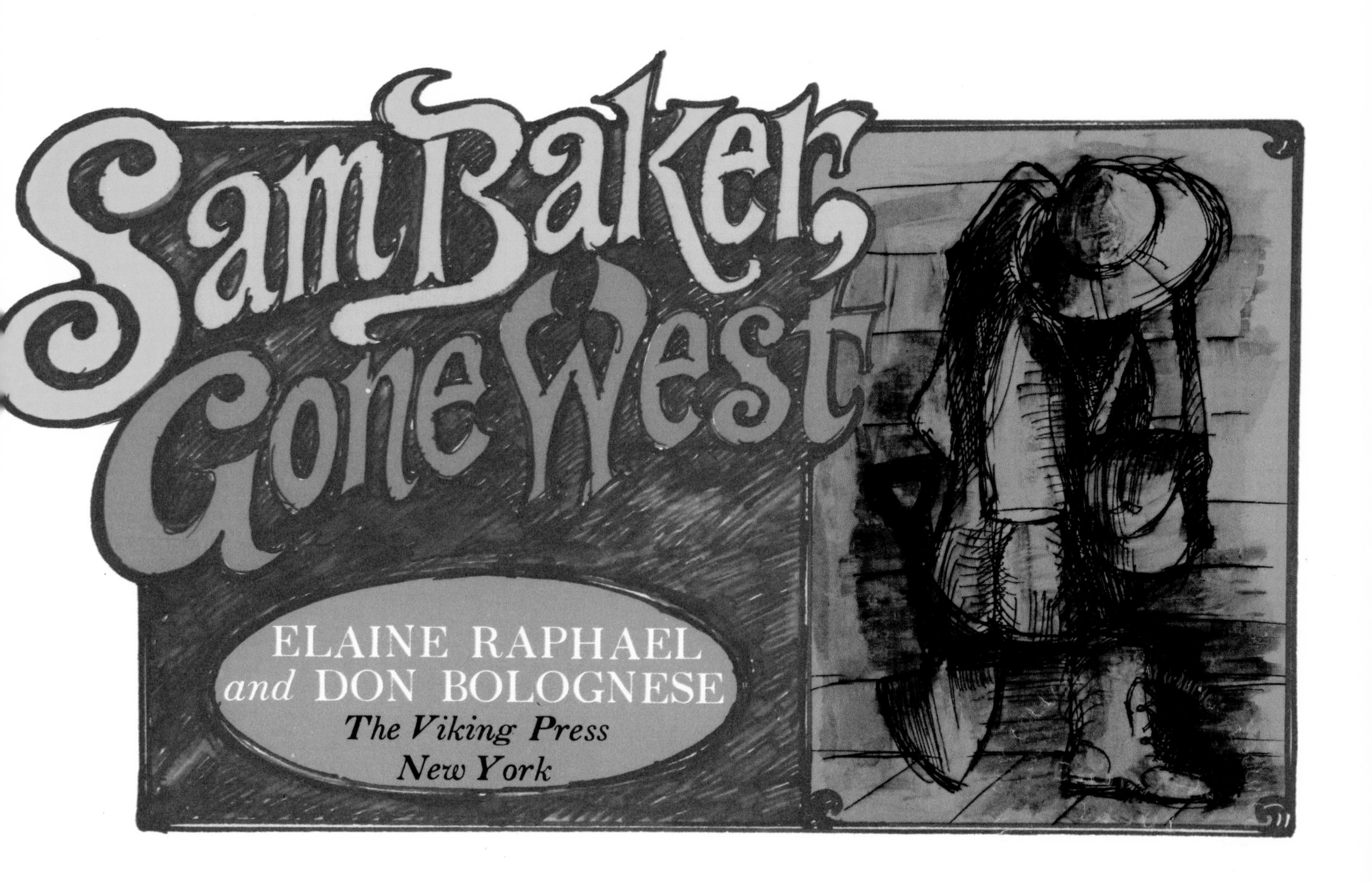
Sam Baker
Gone West
ELAINE RAPHAEL
and DON BOLOGNESE
The Viking Press
New York

FIRST EDITION

First published in 1977 by The Viking Press
625 Madison Avenue, New York, N.Y. 10022
Published simultaneously in Canada by
The Macmillan Company of Canada Limited
Printed in U.S.A.

1 2 3 4 5 81 80 79 78 77

Library of Congress Cataloging in Publication Data
Raphael, Elaine. Sam Baker, gone West.
Summary: Sam Baker's desire for more land
leads him to make a fateful deal with the Indians.
[1. Western stories] I. Bolognese, Don, joint author.
II. Title. PZ7.R1812Sam [E] 76–27314

ISBN 0–670–61651–6

To Earl Loomis for his caring

Sam Baker was a mountain of a man. As he boldly walked across the land, his homespun clothes strained at the seams. He stopped, and his fierce eyes swept over his small farm. Suddenly, Sam's voice boomed and rolled across the fields like thunder.

"Son."

A boy dropped a sack of grain and turned toward Sam.

"Yes, Pa?" he called.

"This fence needs mending. If neighbor Jenkins' cows get in here one more time, there'll be the devil to pay. And tell your brother to bring the team and wagon to the north pasture. I mean to have that hay cut by nightfall."

"Yes, Pa, by nightfall," his son repeated.

Sam walked past him to the barn. He flung open the heavy doors.

"Haven't you finished yet, woman? Where's my breakfast? I can't work on an empty stomach."

"I'm sorry, Sam," his wife answered. "With the extra cows, the milking takes more time."

"Nonsense, woman! And next year? When I have more cows? Will I get my breakfast at noon?"

Sam laughed at his own joke. He slammed the door behind him. Mrs. Baker sighed and went back to her chores.

At supper, Sam ate like a bear. He had the temper of one, too.

"Land," he growled. "I always hear about it too late. Seth Parker just bought a hundred acres; Otis Hart, two hundred. Jake Smith got four hundred acres for a song. And what do I have? A measly forty!"

He tore off a large hunk of bread with his teeth.

"Land. I need more land!" He slammed his fist on the table.

His family sat very still. They stared at their food, too frightened to eat or speak. They had been through this many times before. Sam was silent now. But he had decided: tomorrow he would go to town to ask about land.

Home
Sweet Home

The next day, before dawn, Sam hitched up his team and set out. As he passed his neighbors' farms, he grumbled. "It's unfair; I'm a better farmer than any of them. Why should they have more land?"

Suddenly an infernal rattling interrupted his thoughts.

"Hello there, friend," a deep voice called from the darkness.

Sam pulled up his team. "Greetings," he answered. "Where are you bound for, stranger?"

"To town, friend," a peddler answered with an odd grin. "Been out West for a year, and I'm itching to get back to civilization."

Sam's eyes widened. "The West? What's it like out there? Is there much land?"

"Land? Ha!" The peddler cackled. "That's about all there is. Land and buffalo and more land. And believe me, my friend, it's rich land. I ain't never seen grass so tall. But right now my mouth is watering for real cooking and lively talk. I got a trunkful of tales. Look for me in Cooper's store if you want to hear about it." With that, he snapped his whip, and the horse and wagon bolted away, pots and pans clanging and banging to wake the dead.

POTS & PANS
TOOLS
SOAPS SUNDRIES

Sam looked after him. His mouth hung open. He sat there for a while, thinking. Then, remembering where he was, he shouted to his team: "Hey, there. Get a move on."

When Sam got into town, he raced to the store. He looked up and down the counter and around the room—no peddler.

Disappointed, Sam started to leave, but as he went past a cluster of people, he heard a deep voice.

"Free land, yessir, that's what I said—land for the taking. Land to grow corn high enough to hang your hat."

Sam stopped short. He shouldered his way toward the voice.

"The richest land I ever seen." A trapper was talking.

"Where is this free land?" Sam blurted out.

"Right here," the trapper said. He pointed to an X on a map. "It's about five to six weeks by wagon with a good team and fair weather."

"Who owns it?" Sam asked.

The trapper scratched at his beard.

"Nobody," he answered. "Except Indians. They hunt and trap on it, but they ain't farmers. That land don't mean a thing to them. Why, I heard that they'll give you all you want for next to nothing."

CANDY
FAIR

Sam quickly sketched a copy of the map.

"This bend in the river is where the Indians make camp." The trapper marked the spot with a greasy thumbprint.

"Thanks. I'm mighty grateful," Sam said. He stuffed the map into his leather pouch and rushed out of the store.

"My pleasure," answered the trapper. But Sam was already gone. By the time Sam drove the team through the gate his plans were made.

"West, we're going west," he told his family. "We'll sell everything but the best cows and horses. The house, the barn, the crops, the land—all of it. We can't waste a minute. We got to reach the plains while the good weather holds."

His wife pleaded with Sam to stay. His sons begged. But Sam wouldn't listen. In a week's time he was ready. The wagon was loaded, the team hitched. Sam climbed onto the driver's seat. His family got in. Mrs. Baker turned for a last look at her home. Tears ran down her face. The two boys hung their heads.

Sam snapped the reins. The horse and wagon leaped out of the yard. "At last!" he shouted. "I'm going to have all the land I need!"

The family traveled far. They rode through new and beautiful country; Sam never noticed. With one eye on the sun and another on the map, he headed straight for the Indian camp. Nothing would stop him. He was a man possessed.

Then, at the end of the sixth week, a wheel hit a rock. There was a loud snap, and the wagon pitched to one side.

Sam jumped from the seat. "The devil take it! A broken axle. It'll take three days to fix. I can't wait that long," Sam said.

He saddled up his fastest horse and loaded another with gifts. He looked at his family. "Those Indians can't be more than a hard day's ride from here. You fix the axle and catch up with me."

He wheeled the horses around and galloped off.

By sunset that day Sam was riding into the Indian camp.

Everyone came out to welcome him. After Sam dismounted, the men led him into a tent. They all sat in a circle. The Indians looked at Sam with curiosity. Sam asked for the Chief. One of the men pointed to the tent opening. A man wearing a fox headdress appeared. It was the Chief.

Sam immediately unpacked the gifts and gave them to the Indians. He handed the best one, a shiny steel hunting knife to the Chief. The men were delighted with the gifts and eagerly passed them back and forth. The Chief signaled for silence. Sam waited for the Chief to speak.

"Welcome to our camp," the Chief said. "Your gifts show

that you come as a friend." He paused. Sam held his breath. Again the chief spoke: "We want to show our friendship, too. What can we give you in return?"

Sam could hardly keep still.

The Chief continued. "A fast pony? Some buffalo hides?" The Chief hesitated; then, in a deeper voice he added: "Some land perhaps?"

Sam couldn't be quiet any longer. "Yes, yes, land!" he said. "A little land. That would be best. You seem to have so much."

"Good," said the Chief. "It is done. You can choose your land tomorrow."

That night Sam couldn't sleep for a long time. Plan after plan raced through his brain. "Should I have two hundred acres for corn, or three hundred? And wheat—one hundred? No, much more. And the cattle—some dairy, but beef, too. And, of course, horses."

Exhausted, he finally fell asleep. Hardly had his eyes closed, however, when he began to dream.

He was walking through endless fields of wheat. The peddler floated in the air above them. He wore a huge grin and motioned to Sam.

Suddenly the peddler became the trapper; he, too, smiled at Sam and beckoned to him.

Then the Chief appeared, in the trapper's place, waving and calling to Sam.

Sam woke up with a start. A woman was shaking his shoulder and calling his name. The purple of night had become the blue-green of early morning. It was time.

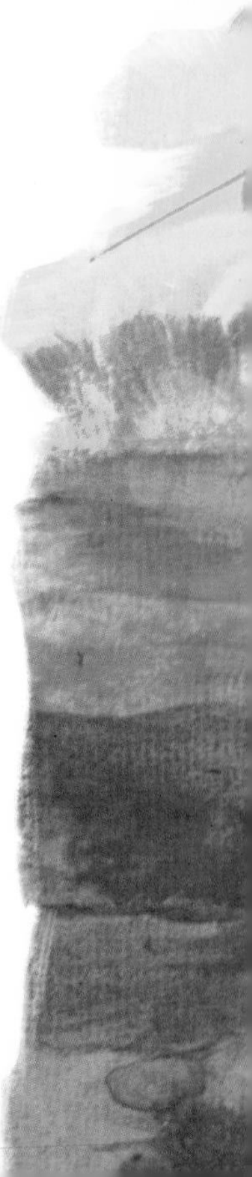

The sky was aglow as they climbed a hill. When they were gathered in one spot, the Chief came up to Sam and stretched his arm toward the plain.

"Look," he said, "all this, as far as your eye can reach, is ours. You may have any part of it which you can walk around in one day."

Sam's eyes glistened; it was all rich, dark, fertile soil.

The Chief took off his fox headdress. He placed it on the ground carefully. "This is the mark. Start from here, and return to this place before the sun sets."

Sam nodded and smiled at the Chief. He put a bag of biscuits in his pouch, tied a flask of water to his belt, and took a shovel from his saddle pack.

He stood and thought for some moments about which way to go.

"I will go south," he said.

The tip of the sun had hardly flashed above the horizon as Sam began. After about a thousand yards, he stopped, dug a hole, and placed a shovelful of earth to mark a boundary.

Sam looked back. He could see the Indians sitting on the hill. It was growing warmer. He took off his coat, flung it over his shoulder, and went on again.

It had grown quite warm now. He looked at the sun, which was well above the hill. It was time to have some breakfast.

"The first side is done—but maybe it's still too soon to turn. I'll go on for just another three miles or so and then turn to the left. This spot is so perfect for corn that it would be a pity to lose any of it. And the farther I go, the better the land gets."

He took off his boots. They were too heavy. He walked another four miles and then turned and headed east to mark off the second side. The sun beat down fiercely. It was right over

Sam's head. He stopped and looked back at the hill. He could barely see it in the haze.

"Have I gone too far? No, I'll keep on in this direction a little longer. I must have this piece; it's perfect for wheat."

He ate as he walked. But now the walking was more difficult. The high grass seemed to push against him. Tangled roots tore at his feet.

Sam longed to stop, but the sun had passed its zenith; it was time to turn again, to mark off the third side.

He headed north. He began to hurry. His legs felt like lead weights.

"What shall I do?" He thought for a moment. "I've got to push on. I can't turn west yet; I haven't gone far enough. The piece of land will be lopsided."

He looked up. The sun was halfway down to the horizon. He felt a stab of fear.

"I've got to turn," he said aloud. He dug another hole to mark his land. He headed west for the hill. It shimmered in the afternoon heat. It was far away.

Sam walked faster and faster. He began to run; he threw away his coat, his pouch, and his boots.

"What shall I do? I can't get there in time," he cried.

Fear made him breathless. He kept running. His sweat-soaked shirt stuck to him. His mouth was parched. His heart was beating like a hammer. His legs, it seemed, didn't belong to him any more.

Sam was seized with terror. Was it all lost?

"What if I'm too late?" he said to himself. His knees trembled. He couldn't stand up.

He looked toward the hill. The sun was touching the rim!

He ran. He was close enough to the hill to hear the Indians yelling to him.

The sun was low now. In the mist it looked large and red. It was about to set. But he was almost to his goal! He could see the fox headdress on the ground.

Sam looked at the sun; a piece of it had disappeared. He ran faster. He had reached the base of the hill when suddenly it grew dark. He looked up: the sun had set. He cried out, "It is all for nothing! I have lost my land."

His legs buckled. He fell to his knees. The Indians were shouting and pointing. The Indians on the hill could still see the sun. There was time! He staggered to his feet and struggled up the slope, his heart pounding. His head throbbed. His breath was thick and fast.

With one last mighty effort Sam reached the top of the hill. He saw the headdress and the Chief. Sam cried out. His legs gave way. He fell forward. He stretched out his arms. The tips of his fingers touched the headdress. He had won his land!

"Ah, that's a fine fellow!" exclaimed the Chief. "You have gained much land."

The Indians gathered around Sam. One of the men lifted Sam's head and looked into his face.

Sam was dead. The Chief looked down at Sam's body and shook his head. He gave a sign. One of his men took Sam's shovel and began digging a grave.

"Make it six feet long from head to heel," the Chief said. "Now he has all the land a man needs."

ABOUT THE AUTHORS AND ILLUSTRATORS

ELAINE RAPHAEL and DON BOLOGNESE met while they were both students at Cooper Union Art School in New York City. They have worked as an artist-writer team, as well as separately, on many art projects and books over the years. Elaine Raphael has been an art therapist in nursery schools and has taught at The Cloisters, part of the Metropolitan Museum of Art in New York. Don Bolognese has taught at the Pratt Institute, Cooper Union, and New York University. They recently collaborated on the illustrations for *Letters to Horseface*, a biography of the young Mozart, by F. N. Monjo.

About *Sam Baker, Gone West*, Raphael and Bolognese say, "We first encountered Western art through the work of such artists as Frederick Remington and Charles P. Russell. But it was the lesser known artists, Carl Bodmer and Rudolph Friederich Kurz, who inspired us for this book.

"These artists-explorers faced the mysterious wilderness of the new

West with sketchbooks and canvas. They brought back portraits of a faraway people—Indians, pioneers, mountain men, and trappers. They also left us stories of a colorful time which produced the myths and legends that have deeply influenced American life. We have tried to capture in our art work the color, space, and energy that is characteristic of Western art."

ABOUT THIS BOOK

The text type used in *Sam Baker, Gone West* is Scotch Roman, set in linotype, and the display type face is Scotch Monotype.

The art work was done in mixed media—pen and ink drawings with washes of acrylic paints, finished with glazes of color. The four-color art was camera separated; the two-color art was separated by the artists. Printed by offset, the book is bound in cloth over boards and has a reinforced binding.

UNDER MY WINGS

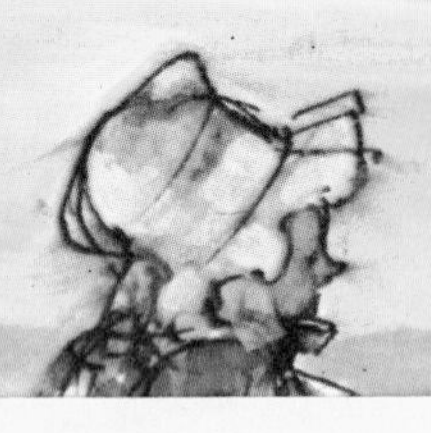